MISSISSIPPI RIVER MUSEUM

MISSISSIPPI RIVER MUSEUM

KEITH PILAPIL LESMEISTER

wtaw press

Edited by Peg Alford Pursell
Designed by Sue Balcer
Cover image: Untitled Collage based on photographs by Sergeĭ Mikhaĭlovich Prokudin-Gorskiĭ, color rendering by Walter A. Frankhauser, Library of Congress, Prints & Photographs Division, Prokudin-Gorskii Collection.

Library of Congress Cataloging-in-Publication data is on file with the Library of Congress.

Lesmeister, Keith Pilapil.
Mississippi River Museum / Keith Pilapil Lesmeister
ISBN 978-1-7329820-7-9 (paperback) | 978-1-7329820-8-6 (ebook)

Published by WTAW Press
PO Box 2825
Santa Rosa, CA 95405
www.wtawpress.org

WTAW Press is a not-for-profit literary press. We are grateful for the assistance we receive from individual donors, public arts agencies, and private foundations.

CALIFORNIA
ARTS COUNCIL
A STATE AGENCY

IN THE FAR CORNER OF NORTHEAST IOWA, WHERE the land slopes into steep ravines and rises up sharp and fast to form rocky bluffs, Joe Patterson lay motionless on a cot in the living room. Saturday morning, late October, he was awake. The air, warm and dry. His body ached from high school sports injuries long past. A spinal concussion, broken ankle, partially torn quadriceps tendon, fully torn rotator cuff. The back of his eyes burst with needles of pain every time his gaze shifted slightly. He could barely straighten his left knee which had bent and stiffened from a poor night's sleep. The smell of sardines reminded him of the night before, when he'd arrived at the cabin. He'd eaten them with a handful of Ritz crackers, both of which he'd found in the kitchen cupboard. He spotted the empty aluminum container sitting on the card table pushed against the wall, its top curled open, still attached. His tongue felt rough and dry, but his water canteen sat on the thin carpet, just out of reach.

He lay there, trying to rub the pain out of his temples and forehead. His lower back was numb. But there'd been no bed to sleep on. Evidently, in the many months since he'd last visited, both twin mattresses and the queen had been hauled out, and this green military-issued cot was the only thing left. He'd moved it into the living room to avoid sleeping in the small, claustrophobic bedrooms.

The house, or cabin, as his father had referred to it, located in the one-square-mile town of Lansing, looked out over the slow-moving Mississippi, and across the muddy stream was Wisconsin, where Joe had received a speeding ticket for one hundred and forty-four dollars yesterday, and with Wisconsin's pay-on-the-spot enforcement, the fine had left his checking account looking like the bottom of a drained shot glass.

The cabin was ten years old, mostly built by his father and him. Joe had been twenty then, just learning some carpentry skills. They had only finished what they could afford, and while water was hooked up to the house, they'd never plumbed it inside. They'd purchased a compost toilet, and brought along gallon jugs of water. Who needed water when cheap beer was the weekend drink of choice? And the cabin was essentially that: a weekend getaway. His father's idea after Joe's mother died of kidney disease. His father said he wanted to spend his weekends in peace, but the truth was, his father didn't want people in his Madison neighborhood to see him stumbling home from the tavern, so he crossed over into Iowa and built the small house on a small crest amongst a row of residential houses that overlooked the longest river in the country. Now, Joe, with the death of his father and a severe need for cash, resolved to fix the cabin — the house — which was to say, plumb in a hot water heater and some fixtures, and sell it.

His situation had grown desperate a few weeks ago after he'd gone to work with a severe hangover, used a pipe cutter on the copper water supply sticking out of the wall in a newly finished bathroom in a newly built house in a newly established housing development in a place called Bowman Woods or Woodland Acres or some such, but had failed to turn off the correct water lever in the unfinished basement. Water shot steadily into the new bathroom while he raced downstairs to search for the right lever, which was in the right place, just difficult to find because it was fairly dark, and darker still with the sizable hangover that kept his eyes half closed. The entire bathroom floor had flooded. He sopped up the water with rags and ripped up the vinyl flooring but not only were the floorboards soaked, so were the bottom three inches of the sheetrock. He didn't have that kind of money to replace any of it, and given that he was still an apprentice, he was like a rookie receiver who drops a pass in an NFL preseason game. He didn't need to hear from the foreman. He quit, left a voice message saying so, and went on his way.

It wasn't that big a deal. Life happens, life goes on. But it was the straw for his fiancé, who'd heard from her friend at the gas station that Joe had been "kind of seeing" some middle-aged mom with a "big saggy ass," which wasn't true. In defending himself, where he'd failed was saying that the woman's ass didn't look that bad. He explained to Summer what had happened: he'd helped the woman who was broke down on the side of the road with an easy-to-fix flat. Though he'd put the spare on in record time, under ten minutes, it had been long enough for Stacy at the Speed-n-Go to see him and tell Summer. That, then losing his job.

Joe asked for the ring back, which had cost him a few weeks' worth of paychecks back when he worked for Afro Auto Body (Big Ben's Auto was its actual name, though no one used it). Joe had liked Afro's but wanted to try the plumbing apprenticeship where he could make more money eventually. If he and Summer were to ever buy a house and start a family. He'd always wanted kids. He was a natural with young people. Volunteered at the YMCA open gym on Saturday afternoons until his knees and lower back started to give out around the age of twenty-eight.

Summer held onto the ring, saying she was still "thinking about things," and when Joe returned to Afro's to see about his old job, Benjamin said, "Sorry, man, but I already hired some young fool."

He'd sat around his apartment for three days getting high on bad weed, half-wittedly contemplating his options: jumping from the highest bridge in the county, piping car exhaust into his sealed vehicle, leaving himself to a bottle of scotch and the elements, before he seriously considered the cabin. On the day he packed up for good, Summer called to say she was reconsidering "for real this time." He said he'd talk to her soon, he had plans to fix up the cabin and sell it, and since she always liked to hear about his industriousness, he thought she'd be pleased, but she'd said, "You're fixing to bang that bitch with the big ass, aren't you?"

He'd sped toward Iowa.

Joe had managed to reach his canteen, his lower back no longer numb from sleeping on the cot but aching. He sipped from the canteen and flipped his phone open. Two missed calls, two texts, and the time: ten a.m. He didn't like sleeping in this long. An echo from his childhood when both parents encouraged him to wake early, to be productive; sleeping in was a mark of laziness. He pushed himself up off the cot, and inspected the two-bedroom house in the morning light. Thin sheet paneling the color of a Tootsie Roll made the living room walls. A free-floating woodstove sat in the corner. Where had that come from? And how was he going to build a chimney?

The Formica countertops in the kitchen had been cut and spliced together and the brown faux-wood cupboards, too, were piecemealed together. The stove and fridge were unplugged, and cobwebs dangled from the ceiling fan. The olive-green carpets in the dust-filled bedrooms were commercial-thin, and he remembered arguing with his dad about how much cozier and nicer it would be if he'd put in carpet padding. He'd gone so far as to say, "Mom would've chosen floor padding." His father didn't budge. Too expensive. But Joe liked the house's overall layout. It was simple. Living room and kitchen in front, bathroom accessible from a door just off the living room, and the two bedrooms tucked into a short hallway behind the kitchen.

The one thing that seemed okay was the composting toilet. A full bag of pinewood shavings stood next to it so they could be dumped in after someone's use. A bath and shower surround kit had been shoved not-so-neatly into the area reserved for one, but absent any handles or hardware, not even the limp-dick-metal-shower piece he'd need to attach the showerhead.

They'd built the cabin after Joe's mother had died, and though he couldn't say for sure, perhaps it was the one reason he'd never felt at home here. It lacked his mother's presence: her smell, her decorative touch, not a single sweater, pair of slip-ons, purse hanging from a door knob. Those things had lingered in their former home, the one he'd grown up in in Madison, long after she'd died. But his father had loved this place, and every time he and Joe talked, it was always, "When are you stopping by the cabin, son?" "Cabin" conjured images of a wooded setting on a clear blue lake in northern Minnesota. This was just a hovel perched next to a muddy river, but that was typical of his father to make things sound better than they were. Joe had rarely visited.

In the bedroom next door to the bathroom, which his father had dubbed "Joe's place," he tore a piece of cardboard from the top flap of one of the boxes scattered across the room and wrote a list of things he needed to purchase at the hardware store. The box held receipts, photos, old documents he had no use for. He'd go through those boxes later, maybe.

Joe stretched before walking to the store, trying to loosen up, a habit he'd developed as a high school basketball and football player. The morning ritual helped to ease some of his low back and neck pain. He reached his arms high, fingertips to the Lord, as his mother used to sing. Joe wasn't a religious man, not anymore, but he sometimes found himself humming along to his mother's favorite hymns: *How Great Thou Art, Come Thou Fount of Every Blessing.* He touched his toes, shook his legs out, one at a time, and skipped out of the bedroom into the living room where he made a few circles around the cot to get the blood moving.

It was a mile walk into town, but the movement helped ease the pain in his joints, and Joe clipped along. He pulled his Brewers hat low to shade against the sun, and arrived uptown in fifteen minutes, the sidewalks crowded with people enjoying sidewalk sales. The biggest crowd gathered outside Be You Antiques.

Inside, the hardware store smelled of paint and varnish and some other odor he couldn't identify but made his headache worse. Joe had been inside the store too many times to count, and wished he'd never had to make another trip, but there he was.

"You look like shit," said the guy at the counter. "Where the hell'd you party last night?" He was an older man, white hair and beard, a Carhartt hoodie and jeans. A sheathed bowie knife hung from his belt.

"No, sir," Joe said. "Just under the weather. Been feeling it for the last few...days, I guess."

"What brings a young buck like you to town during the off-season?"

"Off-season? Oh, tourists. Yeah, my old man had a place up on River Road. I'm here to get a little work done."

"Who's that? Your dad?"

"Patterson. Where can I get some copper and soldering supplies? Need a torch and—"

"Gonna sweat some pipes, are ya?"

"That's the plan."

"Aisle four. Sorry to hear about your dad. He came around every once in a while."

"Like all the time." It was his father's way to escape, to avoid dealing with his mother's passing. A place for his father to run to, to hide, when all Joe wanted was to figure out how to stop crying every night from missing his mother. It had confused him: he didn't think it was normal for a grown ass man to be crying all the time, which is why he never left his apartment. His father had fled to Iowa when Joe needed him most.

"Just when he needed to see ol' Prisilla up there on the hill, his girlfriend," the clerk said.

"Prisilla?" Since his father's death, Joe was becoming more of aware of how separate their lives had been.

"You didn't know about her? Well, I don't know, maybe he didn't use the word 'girlfriend.' "

Another customer came in, and the clerk's attention left Joe.

Back at the house, Joe set his bag of hardware on the round kitchen table, and removed his hat and wiped his damp forehead with the back of his hand before replacing it. He went out the back door onto the patio. The bricks had gone crooked and dead stalks of grass and weeds pushed through the sand-filled cracks. Box elder bugs swarmed him and Asian beetles crawled over the doorframe. A weathered wooden privacy fence enclosed the backyard, one that he'd helped install, and it too wasn't as true as it had been back then. He'd thought helping his father would be a good time to talk—nothing in particular, just the things people talk about, though he also had a desire to reminisce about his mother, something his father hadn't—but they'd only argued about how to put up the fence. Joe wanted to do it right, his father just wanted it done. Didn't care about level and plumb. Any extra effort Joe had made hadn't lasted, he saw now.

He looked over the weedy backyard, hot sun on the back of his neck, and the reality of how much work the property needed was sinking in. Far more than simply plumbing in fixtures.

It was warm for October and Joe wanted to be outside—away from the house. Prisilla, huh? He set off to walk by the river, shimmering in the near distance just across the street. Taking off his sweatshirt and draping it over a shoulder, he crossed the street and the steep grassy embankment to the strip of sand and rock beach skinnier than a two lane highway. A few boats trolled through the channel. Just ahead, a kid with a smoke in his mouth squatted next to a beat-up black and gold GT. "Hey man," he said. "Trying to get my chain back on. Can you help?"

Joe tried to process the kid's age. He looked young, way young, maybe twelve. Maybe. Too young to be smoking.

The kid caught Joe staring. "My girlfriend's outta town. Gotta smoke them while she's gone. She hates this shit." His dark hair was shaved into a crew cut, the kind Joe remembered his dad giving him as a kid. Joe had always hated how his short hair never lay on his head like he wanted. The kid stood and flicked the butt into the river.

Joe examined the GT. A three-speed with four freestyle pegs. A light, durable frame. "The gear shifts are rusty, so is the chain. You got anything like WD-40? Or better yet, some kind of oil?"

"Maybe at the house," the kid said. "Where you stay?"

Joe pointed down the street toward his dad's cabin.

"Old man Patterson's place?"

"You knew him?"

"Everyone did. Dude was off his rocker. He tried to hug my mom every time we saw him at the grocery or the gas station. Always handing out candy and shit. You buy his place? I heard he stroked out a while back."

"No."

"Just staying there?"

"Something like that. Trying to fix it up."

"Yeah, that place needs it." The kid grabbed the handle bars and walked in the direction of Joe's place. "I'm just a couple doors down from you."

Joe found himself following the kid. Maybe it was because the task at hand was an easy fix, or maybe because the kid was about the same age as the team of kids he used to coach at the Y.

"I'm Christian," the kid said, looking back at him.

"Joe."

"Thanks for the help, man," Christian said.

"I haven't done anything yet."

"You look like a guy who gets shit done."

"We'll see," Joe said.

They passed Joe's and headed for a ramshackle house with peeling paint. The roof was missing shingles here and there, and a leash was tied around a good-sized maple whose red leaves lay underneath. Christian led him to the garage in back.

"Hey, who the fuck are you?"

Joe snapped his head around. A woman in a lavender terry cloth robe stood on the concrete stoop outside the backdoor. No slippers, no shoes. Her toenails painted the same color as the old robe, which hung loose on her frame. She was slender, with shoulder-length brown hair she tossed back from her face when she saw she had his attention. She leaned against the door, one arm crossed over her chest, propping the elbow of her other so she had easy access to the cigarette hanging from her hand, inches from her face.

"He's gonna help fix my bike," Christian said.

"You ain't no child molester, are you?"

"No, ma'am," Joe said.

"It's Denise," she said.

"Joe." He offered his hand, but she just looked at it.

"You a Puerto Rican? I've dated Puerto Ricans." She smirked, maybe winked at him. He wasn't sure. She couldn't have been much older than him, but she had noticeable lines around her eyes and a voice that crackled from years of smoking.

"Nah, my mom's from the Philippines."

"Wait," Christian said. "Old man Patterson was your dad?"

"How'd you put that together?" Joe said.

"He told me once about his wife," Christian said. "Said she was an 'exotic treasure from southeast Asia.' "

"Sounds like my old man."

"Didn't know he had himself a half-breed kid," Denise said. She coughed into her hand and pulled her robe tighter.

"Damn, haven't heard that one in a while," he said.

"You ain't gonna get sensitive on me, are you?" she said.

"I'm all right," Joe said.

In the garage, he and Christian got the chain oiled up and reattached to the derailleur. While the bike was propped on its handlebars and seat, Joe cranked the pedals and added more oil until the squeaking stopped. The garage was a single stall with a work bench in back, stacked with a mess of tools spread everywhere. A push mower and two old seventies style twelve speeds stood on kickstands in the middle. The place smelled of gas and cat piss.

"This ain't a bad bike," Joe said. "You keep it oiled up, it'll do okay. You know any tricks?"

"I got a decent wheelie, and check out these pegs."

"I noticed. That's why I asked. I used to have one similar, but all I could do was ramp off curbs. I had a friend who could wheelie all the way down the street. I was always jealous of that."

"I've had it since I was five. That's probably why it's looking a little old. You know what a California bunny hop is?"

"Heard of it, never tried it."

The kid set the bike on its wheels. He hopped on and pedaled on the uneven driveway. He stood on the pedals, readying himself for a trick, and then the back tire went a foot in the air and came back down."

"Not too shabby," Joe said.

"I've been working on it." Christian kept riding around the driveway. "Key is to tap the front brake while you try to bring the back wheel up. Gives you a few extra inches." He got off the bike. It didn't have a kickstand, so he laid it in the grass.

Denise came out the backdoor.

"Joe fixed the bike," Christian said.

She ignored him and presented a plate to Joe with a close-mouthed smile. A ham and cheese sandwich cut diagonally, a pickle spear lying next to it.

Christian reached for a piece of sandwich, but she raised her hand as if to backhand him. He flinched and fell back into the side of the garage.

"Boy, you let our guest eat first," she said.

Christian cowered next to the wall. Joe glared at Denise. A look of surprise and anger, he imagined, was on his face. She stretched the plate in his direction.

"Half is enough for me," he said, taking both and offering the other to Christian, who looked at Denise.

"It's fine, go ahead," she said, sounding annoyed.

Joe gave him the pickle too.

Denise smoked another cigarette while they ate. She picked up the empty plate. "Got to get ready for work," she said.

"Where's that?" Joe said.

"Saloon up the road."

"I heard that place is decent."

"The food's okay," Christian said, sitting on his bike, ready to pedal somewhere.

"Who asked you?" Denise said. "Food's good, beer's good. Make a shit load of tips during season."

"You mean tourist season?"

"Any season. Fishing, hunting, tourist."

"Maybe I'll stop by later if I get enough work done around the house."

"We should go fishing instead," Christian said.

Denise stepped close and patted Joe on the chest. "Stop by. It'll be a party."

"Yeah? What's the occasion? Halloween?"

"No occasion," she said. "But you look like you could use a little fun."

Later that day, Joe was fiddling with the light fixtures in the living room when he saw through the front window the kid's bike on the overgrown lawn. Someone rapped on the door. Christian, no doubt.

Joe opened the door a crack. "What's up?"

"You wanna go fishing off the side of the wall?"

"What wall?"

"There's a place over by Henry's bait shop where you can sit on the ledge and fish with a bobber."

"Sounds nice."

"It is."

"I'm doing a few things, maybe I'll join you after."

"You going up to the Saloon tonight?"

"Don't think so."

"Denise's boyfriend'll probably show up. He's a hillrod from some place up river."

"Good to know."

"He busted me up pretty good one night. Backhanded me real good. His knuckles were like stones. Knocked this tooth clean out." The kid smiled to show his missing eyetooth. He closed his lips and backed away from the door. Joe pictured the way Denise had raised her hand to Christian in the garage earlier.

"I'll let you know if fish are biting, if you don't come."

"Yeah, do that. And good luck."

"And thanks for helping with my bike." The kid put his fist out, and he and Joe bumped.

"Anytime, kid, and maybe you can show me how to bunny hop sometime."

"You're getting a little old for that, aren't you?"

"Come on, man! I'm not *that* old."

Christian laughed. "Yeah, we'll see."

Joe started in on one of the bedrooms, figuring he could seal it off from the other parts of the house while fixing things. He ripped up the carpet, matted and stained and smelling like wet animals and fish scales. Outside, kids rode up and down the street on dirt bikes in the otherwise quiet. He enjoyed this, he realized: the uneventful, small town life. The solitude. More peaceful than the city. Less noise, people.

He went to the bathroom. Next to the compost toilet still sat the original toilet, unattached, dry and empty. Earlier he'd found a new one in the garage, a commercial grade beauty his dad had kept telling himself he'd hire someone to install. Joe carried the old one outside and heaved it onto the front lawn.

"Classy." There was Denise, passing by just then.

"I'll probably move it."

"Not before the neighbors judge your decorating ability."

"Fuck 'em," he said.

"That's what I say. Fuck 'em all."

She strutted up the sidewalk in cowboy boots and jeans, headed in the direction of The Saloon. He cleared the dust off his silver Casio watch, one of his father's watches he'd given Joe for helping him build the house. Even though it had already been old and scratched, he liked it. Midafternoon already, but he'd gotten a lot done.

In the bathroom, he set the wax seal around the main drain, and remounted the new toilet he'd carried in from the garage. It sat high and shiny and already improved the bathroom. He connected the water and turned it on, listening as the reservoir filled up. He used a flashlight to check for leaks, squatting, his knees beginning to ache. All good. Next, the sink. But his energy was waning. Taking breaks was important, he used to tell his kids at the Y.

"Already caught a few," Christian called, when he spotted Joe. He was shirtless, the sun beating directly onto his back—onto the yellowish blue, mottled fading colors of bruises, welts.

Joe looked at the muddy water.

"You got a rig?" the boy said. "I could run back and grab you one of mine."

"I probably have one in the truck back at the house," he said. "But I'll save my fishing for another day. Sounds like you've already caught them all."

"Always more to catch."

"Say," he said. "I'm curious, that hillrod stay with you a lot?"

"At the house?"

Joe nodded.

"Few times a week, I guess. But I scared him off last time, told him I'd kill him if he came back around."

"Why's that?"

"He's always poking at Denise, pissing her off. And he drank the rest of my OJ."

Joe chuckled, thinking that's what the kid wanted.

Christian held up a single cigarette. "You need a smoke? I steal 'em from Denise."

"You don't need to smoke in front of me." He remembered this about himself when he was the kid's age, trying to impress older men, smoking, swearing, swigging from beers.

The boy set the cigarette on his tackle box without comment.

A breeze lifted off the muddy water. It didn't smell bad, only like the muddy river it was. People were starting to file in for happy hour at the bar and grill next to Henry's bait shop. Both places were in the same worn-down building with its concrete foundation and shabby wooden planks that acted as a walkway.

Directly across from where Christian was fishing, bald eagles—three of them—soared above the island. The locals called it Hermit Island. A hundred-yard stretch of woods where it was rumored that an old hermit had once lived for fifty years before a group of kayakers discovered him prancing around a beach.

"My old man liked to fish," Joe said. "He would've told you not to fish in the afternoon, the best fishing is early morning or evening. But it looks like you're doing just fine. You ever talk to him, my dad?"

"Now and then," Christian said.

"He ever tell you about the Mississippi River Museum down in Dubuque?" he asked. "Got like hundred-pound catfish swimming around the aquariums, and stuff you've never seen before, prehistoric shit that'll give you the creeps."

"No, he never said nothing about it. I swim in there all the time." Christian nodded toward the river.

"You might not, if you saw all the stuff in that museum."

"You been there?"

"Actually, no. We were supposed to go once, but something happened. But I remember what he told me."

"I'd like to go sometime." The kid pulled up on his rod and reel. "Damn, missed it. Probably a blue gill. So, your mom was from the Philippines, huh?"

"That's right."

"How'd she get over here? How'd they meet—your mom and dad?"

"Military. My dad was in the army, stationed over there. They met, had me, and that's the story."

"You don't look Asian to me."

"How's that?"

"Not so slanty eyed. Don't have that chinky look like some people I've seen."

Joe laughed. "Where'd you hear that shit—slanty and chinky—from Denise?"

"Nah, some movie, I think."

"Pretty sure that's not the right way to describe someone, though." He laughed lightly so the kid wouldn't feel bad.

"So, you're a half-breed too. Like me."

"What do you mean?"

"I'm part Mexican or Hispanic or something. I think my real mom is from Costa Rica or Cuba or maybe Puerto Rico."

The boy's features were dark but not noticeably so. His hair was brownish-black, but his eyes were blue. His skin was a shade darker than average, maybe.

"Where'd you get that word? Half-breed? And real mom, what's that about?"

"That hillrod, all he calls me is half-breed this, half-breed that. 'Hey, half-breed bitch, go get me a beer' or 'hey, half-breed spic, go tell your worthless mother to make me a sandwich.' But she ain't my mom. She's just the woman my dad was with before he took off for wherever. Don't know where, don't know where my real mom is, neither of them."

"That right?" He settled his gaze on two men in a fishing boat not far from shore. One of the guys was struggling to reel in a fish, his rod tip bent toward the water. With a little effort and patience, the guy could land the fish. It was a matter of focus. Keeping the line tight and the drag set perfectly. A balance, a give and take.

"I'd kill that hillrod if I ever got the chance," Christian said. "He told Denise he'd drag her into the woods and choke her out if she ever tried to leave him."

"That right?" Joe said.

“Then he’ll bring her a bottle of Boone’s or some hooch he made up in the hills. Every once in a while, me a soda. Try to make things right.” He shook his head.

Joe looked at the fading bruises on the kid’s back. Rage percolated in his gut. “I got to get back to things,” he said.

Christian nodded and set the hook again.

At home Joe sat on a rickety lawn chair on the uneven brick patio observing the soft light that lingered from sunset on the enclosing hills. He drained two cans of Old Milwaukee and went inside to find something to eat. He rummaged through cupboards where he’d found the sardines the night before and found fruit cocktail and baked beans. He ate both from the can and added going to the store tomorrow to his list of to-dos. In the living room, without much hope, he tried to hook up the dusty TV to the cable outlet. The cable would have been disconnected, but there was a Badger game on he wanted to see.

He put on a stocking cap and buttoned his quilted flannel. The days were warm, but temps plummeted at night, dropping down to forty degrees. He could hop in his truck, a twenty-year-old F150 that used to be his dad’s, but the anonymity of walking in the dark always appealed to him. Joe shoved his hands in his flannel pockets. Main Street was strung with lights, a new touch since he’d last been there, and he liked how they made the town seem bigger than it was.

The Saloon. He peered inside. It was too much: too loud, too many people, and he'd earlier talked himself out of a confrontation with the hillrod, who he wanted to kill as much as Christian did. *Try to make things right.* The kid's voice when he said that. He went down the street to another bar. Inside, the bartender, a guy with a mustache and a hooded sweatshirt, nodded.

Joe scanned the room to see what everyone else was drinking. "Old Style," he said to the barkeep. Halftime and the Badgers were losing by a touchdown.

The following morning, he woke the same way he always did these days—with pain in his head, eyes, back, and shoulders. Hungover. He'd been drinking more, like his father had here in this house. Far more than ever. It offered a temporary relief. But the mornings were getting worse. He twisted from his back to his side on the cot and scanned the floor for his canteen. The house smelled of his father. A smell he couldn't describe, but understood as his father's smell.

It was Sunday, and bells clanged at the Catholic Church on the edge of town. He winced, opening cabinets, every drawer he hadn't already scoured. Nothing. He needed groceries. He had a credit card.

Joe parked in a handicap spot before he noticed the mistake. He reversed the truck and realized his was the only vehicle in the grocery store lot. He squinted at the sign taped to the front door. Closed all day. He parked and went to the Kwik Star across the street. Cheap eggs, cheese, and milk.

Coffee, a loaf of white bread, and turkey and ham cold cuts. Everyone in the gas station—about a half dozen bodies—was sour-faced and smelly from the night before. He figured he looked and smelled the same. All the clean people were in church. He set his basket on the counter. The cashier was a pleasant woman in her early twenties.

"Yeah, I saw you cross the street," she said to Joe. "We get a lot of Sunday traffic on account of their being closed."

"I imagine."

"What brings you to town?"

Joe looked behind him to see who might be listening. He was learning how small towns worked.

"You're visiting, right?" the clerk said.

"Just visiting family."

"Who's that?"

"Just up the road." He avoided making eye contact while the cashier rang him up and bagged his stuff.

Once home, he cooked quickly, robotically, and stood at the counter and forced down a piece of toast and one egg cooked over hard. He sipped the coffee. Too strong. Stirred milk into it and sipped again. Almost right away the caffeine soothed his head. It was another sunny day.

He went about his chores as planned. He pulled up all the carpet and warped linoleum in the house and dragged it to the curb, hoping the garbage collectors would take it whenever they came by. When thoughts about the kid and his mother, or not-mother, popped up, he pushed them away. He'd had a lot of practice pushing away thoughts. Close to dinnertime, there was a knock at the door. Joe slumped against the wall in the bathroom where he'd been working on small stuff: tightening plumbing fixtures, remounting electrical outlet plates. He just wanted to be left alone. Finish his work.

He pulled the front door open just enough to peer through.

It was Denise. Jeans and a tight black V-neck, no shoes. She held a covered paper plate. "Brought you something."

Joe stared at the plate. Whatever it was, it smelled delicious.

"Pork chop," she said.

He hesitated.

"You're not one of those vegetarian types, are you?"

"I'm a meat eater."

"That's what I like to hear."

He took the plate from her and started to close the door.

"You ain't gonna ask me in?"

A glimmer of light reflected off a silver earring dangling from her ear next to her slender neck. Joe hesitated again. Something about those bare feet. Part of him wanted to invite her in. But the way she'd treated the kid. Her raised hand. The kid cowering. "Really messy in here," he said, "but thanks for the food."

He closed the door and leaned against it, ripping the aluminum foil from the plate. He clutched the pork chop by the bone and tore into it, catching the juices with the plate. He stared at the foil on the floor, chewing, unable to do anything about the nagging rage that arose in him. Denise, the hillrod. It was none of his business, and yet it was his business. He felt a gnawing sense of obligation. To the kid.

Over the following days, Joe rechecked his bank balance, which still hovered in the double digits. He needed to list the house pronto. He'd meant only to prep the house to put on the market, but he'd started new projects beyond upgrading the plumbing and painting walls: flooring, patching up electrical, and hooking up the disassembled chimney he'd found in the garage rafters to the woodstove. Ibuprofen barely numbed the aches and pains. Back, neck, shoulders, always his knees—reminders of those quick lateral movements on the court and football field. By Friday afternoon, he got a hankering to call Summer but his phone didn't work well. He loved his flip phone and felt a sense of pride knowing he hadn't bought into the smartphone craze. But here in the valley it didn't matter what phone you had—the signal was weak or nonexistent.

Uptown, a pay phone sat at the edge of the parking lot at the Kwik Star.

"How you doing, babe?" he said.

"I'm okay, what's up? You all right?"

"I'm good. About finished up with my dad's place. Thinking about finding a realtor and scooting back sooner than later."

"You mean coming back here?"

"Yeah, to see you."

"Listen, I don't—"

"Look, don't say anything now. We should talk about this over dinner or something." He was beginning to sense something in her voice.

"That's not going to work."

"Why's that?" She'd been back and forth with one of her ex's early on in their relationship, and it was this same strain in her voice the last time it'd happened. "You ain't back with Ronnie, are you?"

"I'm sorry, but—"

"Man, I've been gone for like a week."

"I should go," she said.

"So that's it?"

"Maybe call me some time," she said.

"The fu—"

But she'd already hung up.

The fuck he would. Call her? The fuck he would. He folded a second pillow under his head on the cot. He lay staring at the ceiling fan he'd installed. What would his father think of the fan? A waste of money, Joe guessed. Had his father ever thought Joe might live here? Had he ever thought Joe might hear of Priscilla? Meet the woman? He sipped bottles of Old Style he'd purchased the day before. He drank until they were gone.

When he walked into the hardware store the next morning, the guy said, "You're still around? I figured you must have took off."

"I'm still here," Joe said. "Barely. I need a cheap rod and reel."

"Well, let's take a look." The man adjusted his trousers and led him to a display at the back of the store. "This here's the cheapest we got." He handed him a spinning reel and rod.

Joe checked the price tag.

"Unless," the man said, "you want the Cartoon/Kids rig. That's the cheapest-cheapest."

Joe's legs dangled over the concrete wall, the water below a swirling eddy of litter and foam and green sludge. He didn't care. He just wanted to fish. He just wanted to catch those small sunnies or blue gills and release them back to their own doings so he could catch them again and again. The sun was beating on the side of his face and he was sweating underneath his shirt. He was ready for cooler weather. Some change to finally mark the season.

He tied a hook to the end of the three-foot-long Snoopy rod and reel, pinched off a section of night crawler and attached it to the hook. He put a bobber on the fishing line and a sinker in between the hook and bobber and dropped the line straight down. A few boats motored by. He wagged his legs back and forth, and the concrete scraped his jeans. It was his father who'd taught him how to fish, when he was a kid. They didn't go often, and his father never caught anything, but he still loved it. He'd said to Joe, "Even when it's bad, it's still good," and chuckled at himself. Joe wondered if others would find it cold and calloused if he admitted he hadn't felt anything since his father's passing. He just wanted to get the house sold and be done with it.

"You catch anything?" Christian rolled up on his bike.

"Nada. Your bike chain staying on?"

"Yeah, no problems." He sat down next to Joe. "Nice rig—Snoopy?"

"It's temporary."

"It's temporarily not catching you any fish." Christian flung his line out past Joe's and the hook, line, sinker, bobber, splashed to a stop.

He smirked, but then noticed bruising around the kid's wrist. Whatever he'd been about to say left him.

They fished without talking. Gulls flew overhead. People biked and walked by, their sneakers scuffing the walkway. More boats motored through the channel. A few kayaks near shore. Joe liked hanging out with the kid, but there was always the burden of knowing what was going on at home. Was he supposed to have a chat with Denise and the hillrod?

"What do you think you wanna be when you get old?" Joe said.

"Old like you?"

He laughed. His bobber went under and popped back up. He pulled up to set the hook, but whatever had tried to take the bait was gone.

"Probably those little ones," Christian said. "They can't take all that bait at once so they just nibble on it. Anyway, maybe a cop."

"A cop?" He laughed again.

"Well, whatever," Christian said. "Soon as I'm old enough to get out on my own, I'm outta here, you know? She's always telling me she'd like me to get the fuck out of her life. There!" He pointed at Joe's bobber and Joe pulled on it instinctively.

He set the hook and felt something really tug on the line. It swam in a figure eight and the tip of the rod bent toward the water. It kept fighting. "Might be a bass," he said.

"Might be a nice one," Christian said.

The fish wore itself out, and he reeled it in and brought it up out of the water.

"Catfish!" Christian said.

It was olive brown with a large head and whiskers, maybe sixteen inches long. He worried the cheap pole might snap, so he secured the line and pulled the fish up hand over hand. Once he got it to the top of the wall, he clutched the catfish behind the side fins and avoided the stingers. "You know about the stingers, right?"

"Of course," Christian said.

Joe offered the catfish to the kid. "You wanna unhook it then?"

"You go ahead." Christian held his hands up and backed away, a mock look of fear on his face.

Joe laughed. "I don't blame you. I've been stung a few times. Hurts like hell. But hey, we're gonna be eating some catfish tonight!"

Christian stood next to Joe on the patio while he hammered a nail through the catfish's head, securing it to a two-by-four.

He set the board on the bricks and dumped boiling water over the body, and started peeling back the skin like a pro, like his father had taught him.

"Haven't done this in a while," he said.

"This place needs help," Christian said. He'd moved over to the patio door and was peering inside where Joe's cot lay in the living room, his tools and hardware spread across the kitchen counter and living room carpet. "But it's looking a little better than the last time I saw it."

"Work-in-progress, my man." He felt pleased with the kid's comment. He was making things better. "You ever eat cat?" he said.

"All the time. Well, sometimes. Denise makes it if the hillrod comes around with a stringer."

"Come on, let's fry this up."

In the kitchen, he rolled the catfish in a store-bought breading, an old package from the cupboard—his dad always kept on hand just in case—while peanut oil heated inside a frying pan. After a few minutes, he flicked water onto the pan and it sizzled.

"Look out!" Christian said, excited by the sound of the oil popping.

Joe laughed.

While the catfish cooked, Christian paced through the house, poking his head into the bathroom, the two bedrooms. In the living room he said, "Wood stove looks nice."

"Thanks, it's a decent addition."

"Can I have your cot when you leave?"

"You don't have a bed?"

"It looks cool. Maybe I can use it if I run off into the hills."

Joe knew what Christian was getting at, but he sniffed the air exaggeratedly. "I think we're about done here. Smells good, huh?"

"Smells great!"

They stood at the Formica countertop eating it with plastic forks, their paper plates soaked to the edges with grease. They ate in silence, and when they finished, the kid burped.

"I could eat another," Christian said.

"Not too bad, if I do say so myself."

Christian said, "How about you? What are you gonna be when you grow up?"

Joe wiped his mouth with a paper napkin. "That too, a work-in-progress." The kid nodded with a look of encouragement. "I guess I thought about going back to school someday. Maybe be a science teacher and coach basketball."

"I don't like kids that much," Christian said. "Kind of annoying, if you ask me."

Joe laughed and tossed his napkin toward the sink like he was shooting a basket.

"Two points!" Christian said. Then he backed up and launched his napkin into the sink and made it.

After Christian had gone, Joe sat on the floor in the living room, the radio tuned to some political talk show that he found horrible, the way the broadcaster's voice emphasized all the wrong words. We will not begin TO understand... or How is IT that our president... He tossed a chewed-up tennis ball, one he'd found in the yard near the neighbor's property, against the wood paneling, pushing thoughts away. Back and forth, thump, smack, thump, smack, until he couldn't sit still any longer.

In the cool dark of evening, he walked along the river-front, aware of the water next to him. A silent flow. While he understood perfectly that the river made some kind of sound—the sound of water moving so slowly as to seem still—he couldn't hear it. He could only sense its presence.

Inside The Saloon, families were just finishing pizzas and pitchers of soda. A row of booths stretched across the far wall, each framed by tall wooden pillars festooned with maroon drapes. A whiskey barrel stood at the end of the bar full of unshelled peanuts, and baskets of them dotted the bar and rested at the edges of the tables. The floor was a mess of broken shells.

"Well, well," Denise said, coming out from behind the bar, her apron folded so it covered her only from the waist down. She wore a halter top with no bra, and later, when she bent over to clean pint glasses behind the bar, he understood why. Her tip jar next to the sink was stuffed full of ones.

"Old Style," he said.

"All business tonight, huh? How's it going?"

"Thirsty."

All the tables were taken and he sat at the bar. A college football game played on the TV above. A few men watched, while some talked to Denise.

A bearded guy said to her, "You seen that boating accident happened the other day?"

"Didn't see it, heard about it though. Heard it was bad."

"Critical condition for all them passengers. Took them up to La Crosse."

"Not even drinking is what I heard."

"Sounds right."

Joe focused his attention on the game and ordered another beer. Then another. A shot of whiskey. He grabbed a handful of peanuts and started eating. The bar filled in around him.

"Them are my peanuts," the guy sitting next to him said.

Joe felt his heartbeat quicken. "Say what?"

"Said those are my peanuts."

Joe grabbed another handful and set them down next to his beer. "Have 'em," he said.

The guy laughed, adjusted his trucker's cap. "Just fucking with you, man."

A sense of annoyed relief washed over him. He wasn't there for a confrontation.

"What brings you to town?" the guy asked.

"Well, look at you two, hitting it off," Denise said. "Need another?"

"Woman, don't interrupt us," the guy said. Then he curled the sides of his mouth upwards as if to suggest a joke. He laughed, showing a dark build up around his teeth.

Denise pretended to ignore him. "So? Another?"

"One more, then I got to roll," Joe said.

“Where you got to go?” the guy said. “Ain’t you the half-breed I heard about staying up at old man Patterson’s place?”

He shook his head. Whenever he heard those words—chink, gook, slant-eyed, or now half-breed—he thought of his grandfather, his father’s father, who used to tote him around in an old Chevy pickup truck, taking him to the animal feed stores and showing him off to his friends. His grandfather would introduce him, “This here is my little chink. Ain’t he something?” After he’d grown older, he was struck by the inaccuracy of his grandfather’s slur and wondered if there were any reserved especially for Filipinos.

The man next to him was annoying but harmless. Then he kept going. “Yeah, heard about you from Denise’s boy, said you helped him with his bike. Worthless little piece of shit, too, that kid. Doesn’t know his ass from a hole in the ground.”

A flash of heat raced through Joe’s arms and legs, momentarily disorienting him. He waved Denise over. “Two Turkeys, straight up.”

“Gonna get wild in here,” she said, and made a gobbling sound.

“One for me, one for him.” They shot Turkey, and Joe ordered another. “On my tab.”

His tongue felt numb and thick. The hillrod hadn’t stopped talking. Joe stared at the man’s knuckles. Tried to imagine him ripping into the kid, into Denise. He was just a skinny methed-out greaser. In his mind, Joe had him built up into something more, some gargantuan monster, some hulk of a man. But he wasn’t that big at all.

Not to Joe. Joe wasn't a skinny twelve-year old kid.

The hillrod jabbered away, to no one in particular, talked down at the empty shot glass—ice fishing, hunting, hiking up in the hills, no one thinks there's bears in Iowa but he'd seen two black bears, different ones, in a matter of just a couple weeks.

Joe interrupted. "I bet you like to fight. Bet you could really pack a punch."

"Not really, I'm not much of a fighter." He opened his mouth and pointed to the gaps, dark spaces where teeth should've been. "Old man knocked out this one and this one. He was the fighter. Jab jab, hook, uppercut. Knocked me out cold several times before I shot him in the knee cap and moved out here."

Joe considered that he was telling the truth.

"You wanna know who's a fighter around here?" The hillrod pointed at Denise, where at the other end of the bar, she was pushing pint glasses up and down into the rotating brushes and stacking them on the counter next to the sink. "That woman's got more fight than a rabid opossum. Beats that boy of hers silly. Ain't even her kid. That kid ain't even hers and she's trying to raise him? What the fuck is wrong with this country? People don't even wanna raise their own goddamn kids."

Joe waved to order two more shots.

"You trying to kill me?" the hillrod said.

"Not yet." Joe clutched the empty shot glass. "But maybe later."

The man chuckled, then coughed into his hand.

"More for ya?" Denise held the bottle of Wild Turkey, made that distorted gobble-gobble sound, and poured two shots. Then, "Open up." The hillrod made like a baby robin and tilted his head back, and she poured a shot's worth in his mouth. She set the bottle down on the bar to regain a better grip and as she did, Joe grabbed her wrist.

"I hear you can really fight," he said.

She tried to pull away, but he held her secure.

She smiled at him. "What's with you?" She looked around to see if anyone was watching.

"You and this loser over here like to hit that boy—maybe you should pick on someone else, huh?" He cinched her wrist tighter. Pulled her closer. Even in the middle of all this, he knew he was flat out drunk.

"You gonna make a scene?" she said.

The hillrod stood, wobbled a bit, and sat back down. "Is there an issue here?"

"Joe's drunk," Denise said. "I can tell." She tried to pull away. "You're hurting me," she said, louder now. Three guys came over from their place at the end of the bar.

"I hope everything's okay over here," one said.

"Everything's fine," Joe said, letting go of Denise's wrist. He got up and went into the bathroom. He splashed water on his face, and dabbed himself dry with paper towels. In the mirror, his eyes were fire engines. He ducked out the front door.

Next morning when he woke, his head felt like a box of ready-mix concrete. He had to wear sunglasses inside the house. The place was at least clean, finally, but the scent of the lemon freshener caused him to vomit into the new toilet. He forced himself to secure the cabin and packed a few things in his duffle bag. He needed to get away from here, just for a while, and then he'd come back to finish things up.

Almost noon. Outside, the sun was high and bright. Joe crossed the street to get a better view of the river. Christian was fishing at the wall, pulling up a blue gill.

Denise, in her robe, was marching down the sidewalk in his direction. Joe crossed back over and set his duffle on the hood of the truck.

"You gotta a helluva bill to pay up at The Saloon," she said. "And you owe me an apology."

"I don't have any money."

"You're gonna get a call from the police chief."

He laughed out loud at the sound of it. "Chief?"

"Only have one officer in town, dip shit," she said.

"Get out of my face," he said.

"You're just like your dad, aren't you?"

"Trying hard not to be."

Christian came running up with a catfish still attached to his line. "Lunch!" he said.

"Not bad," Joe said.

"Where you going?" Christian looked at the duffle bag.

"I was going to leave town for a bit. Need a little break."

"What about this cat?"

"Don't be talking to this piece of shit," Denise said. "Get on home."

Christian glanced at him, and he figured the boy was hoping he would respond, but before he could think what to say, Denise piped up.

"Boy," she said, with a hand up, walking toward him. "Don't defy me."

The boy moved to hide behind Joe.

"What—you think you're not gonna get it the second you come home?"

"Fuck you," the kid said. "I hate you."

"Ungrateful little shit." She tried to grab him, but Joe caught her arms, held her back.

"Go," he said to her. "Leave."

"This is none of your goddamn business," she said. "Don't think we won't press charges for you assaulting me last night. We're not scared of some out-of-towner. Go ahead and play the race card too. We got witnesses."

He let go of her arms. He took off his sunglasses and squinted at her. She backed up.

"I'm too tired to listen to you right now. You need to leave this kid alone."

"You need to mind your own goddamn business," she said. "Little fucker's gonna get it, second he gets home."

Joe said to the kid, "Ignore that shit."

They watched her march up the sidewalk. When she reached the edge of her yard, she shouted, "I'm calling the police!" and disappeared inside the house.

"You all right?" Joe asked.

Christian nodded but looked wide eyed and hesitant.

Joe stood thinking. Once in an overtime playoff basketball game, his coach had said, "Man, you're a natural under pressure. Don't think, Joe. Just do your thing, man. Let that instinct take over. It'll never steer you wrong."

He looked at Christian. "You remember that museum I told you about?"

"With the hundred-pound cats?"

"I'm fixing on driving down there. You want to check it out?"

"Denise ain't gonna let that happen," Christian said. "And you heard her. If I go over there, I'll get it real good. Plus, that hillrod'll take my cat."

"Nah," he said. "You toss that cat back in the river. You remember how to avoid the stingers?"

The kid nodded.

"Good. Then come back and keep an eye on my bag."

"But man, we should try to keep the catfish."

The kid was proud of his catch. "There'll be plenty to catch later, promise," Joe said.

Christian hustled back to the concrete ledge where his bike perched in the dirt nearby.

Joe's head felt worse than ever, but his mind was sharp and efficient, so clear in fact that he felt a moment of what seemed like clairvoyance that buoyed him as he trudged down the sidewalk to Denise's. The boy pulled up next to him on his bike.

"I should go in with you," Christian said.

Something drew Joe's attention away, to the river. There, things had shifted, but he couldn't say how. The sun hit the ripples on the surface and the water appeared a dark sea-blue, as he imagined how the ocean might look.

"You go back and wait at the truck," he said, refocusing. "Just go hang tight. I'll take care of this." At the door he turned around to make sure. The boy was still there, holding his bike.

"Go on now," he said. He rubbed the back of his neck. "We'll be on our way to see those hundred-pound cats in no time. I'm just gonna have some quick words here."

He turned to the door and didn't bother knocking.

The car ride was silent at first. They took the "Scenic Byways" route along the Mississippi, south toward Dubuque. As they wound their way up and down steep hills and valleys, Joe kept telling himself he'd made the right decision, this was what the kid needed. He tried to work out in his mind why Christian was always talking about the hillrod but never Denise. It must have been the kid's way of trying to protect the one person who resembled a parent figure, and maybe he thought the hillrod was to blame for her behavior. Maybe the kid created that narrative in his mind to protect himself from admitting the truth about her.

Eventually, Christian said, "What happened back at the house? They gonna be hunting me down? You think I'm gonna have to go back?"

Joe turned the radio down, a country station he didn't want to listen to, just the only station that would tune in consistently. "Let me ask you," he said, "and be serious with me. Do you want to go back? I'll take you back if you want."

Christian looked out the window. They were winding upward, along the edge of a treelined bluff, where the forest floor would already be covered with a hearty bed of fallen leaves. "I don't," Christian said. "I don't ever wanna go back." He craned his neck to look back in the bed of the truck. "Glad my bike fit."

"For sure," Joe said.

He calculated what time they'd arrive at the museum. Now that the adrenaline had worn off, he was feeling foggy again. But earlier he'd felt sharp, clear and confident, addressing Denise and the hillrod. He'd spoken deliberately and plainly, laid out what he knew—about them, about the kid who was not her kid. He was taking the boy with him on a field trip. Denise said, "What are you going to do? Raise him? I'm the one whose been taking care of the little shit."

"And you're never going to see the kid again, so know this: when I drive past you in a few minutes, if you want to wave bye, that'll be your one chance."

Denise started to cry. "He's my boy!" she screamed. "You know nothing!"

The hillrod held her back from attacking Joe.

"Maybe you're right," Joe said. "And maybe the kid'll decide what happens."

The hillrod put a finger in Joe's face. "Gonna come hunt you down and kill you, you hear me?"

Joe raised his arms in invitation. The hillrod worked his jaw. His eyelids twitched.

Denise shook loose of the hillrod's grip and slapped Joe. She tried again, but Joe blocked her and shoved her toward the hillrod, who caught her. Message delivered, Joe left.

When they drove past the house moments later, he slowed the truck, but there was no one waving in sight. No one at the windows. Only an empty-looking house in need of paint, and a dog's leash hanging from the trunk of a sugar maple.

"So how long's it gonna take for us to get there?" Christian said. A vast unobstructed view of the river emerged now that they'd circled around a bluff. "Can't wait to see those hundred-pound cats!"

"It'll be all right," Joe said, unsure who most needed to hear this. "Been meaning to get there for a while now."

Acknowledgments

Grateful thanks to the wonderful crew at WTAW Press, especially Peg Alford Pursell for her support and editorial patience. I first drafted this story, now chapbook, in the fall of 2015. It feels silly to say a lot has happened since then, but it's true: a lot has happened, and the fact that all these years later this story found a home is humbling. I owe a debt of gratitude to the support and sound advice from those who read early versions of the story: Libby Flores, Denton Loving, Cassie Pruyn, Walter Robinson, and Cathy Salibian. And thanks forever to my family: Molly, Celia, Franklin, and Nora for being tough, wise, and, when needed, light-hearted.

KEITH PILAPIL LESMEISTER is the author of the story collection *We Could've Been Happy Here*. He's a founding editor of *Cutleaf*, a literary journal, and EastOver Press. His fiction has appeared in *American Short Fiction, Gettysburg Review, New Stories from the Midwest, North American Review, SLICE, Terrain.org*, and many others. His nonfiction has appeared in the *Good Men Project, River Teeth, Sycamore Review, Tin House Open Bar, Water~Stone*, and elsewhere. A graduate of the Bennington Writing Seminars, he lives and works in the Driftless region of northeast Iowa.

WTAW Press is a not-for-profit literary press. We are grateful for the assistance we receive from organizations, foundations, and individual donors. We especially wish to thank the following individuals for their sustained support.

Nancy Allen, Lauren Alwan, Robert Ayers, Andrea Barrett, Mary Bonina, Vanessa Bramlett, Harriet Chessman, Melissa Cistaro, Mari Coates, Martha Conway, Michael Croft, Janet S. Crossen, R. Cathay Daniels, Ed Davis, Walt Doll, DB Finnegan, Joan Frank, Helen Fremont, Nancy Garruba, Michelle Georga, Ellen Geohegan, Anne Germanacos and the Germanacos Foundation, Rebecca Godwin, Stephanie Graham, Catherine Grossman, Teresa Burns Gunther, Annie Guthrie, Katie Hafner, Christine Hale, Jo Haraf, Adrianne Harun, Lillian Howan, Yang Huang, Joanna Kalbus, Caroline Kim-Brown, Scott Landers, Ksenija Lakovic, Evan Lavender-Smith, Jeffrey Leong, The Litt Family Foundation, Margot Livesey, Karen Llagas, Nancy Ludmerer, Kevin McIlvoy, Jean Mansen, Sebastian Matthews, Grace Dane Mazur, Kate Milliken, Barbara Moss, Scott Nadelson, Betty Joyce Nash, Miriam Ormae-Jarmer, Cynthia Phoel, John Philipp, Lee Prusik, Gail Reitano, Joan Silber, Charles Smith, Michael C. Smith, Marian Szczepanski, Kendra Tanacea, Karen Terrey, Renee Thompson, Pete Turchi, Genanne Walsh, Judy Walz, Tracy Winn, Rebecca Winterer, Rolf Yngve, Olga Zilberbourg

More titles available from WTAW Press

One Kind Favor: A Novel by Kevin McIlvoy

The Groundhog Forever: A Novel by Henry Hoke

Like Water and Other Stories by Olga Zilberbourg

Chimerica: A Novel by Anita Felicelli

Hungry Ghost Theater: A Novel by Sarah Stone

Unnatural Habitats and Other Stories by Angela Mitchell

And There Was Evening and There Was Morning: A Memoir by Mike Smith

The Truth About Me: Stories by Louise Marburg

WTAW Press provides discounts and auxiliary materials and services for readers. Ebooks are available for purchase at our website book shop. Readers' guides are available for free download from our website. We offer special discounts for all orders of 5 or more books of one title.

Instructors may request examination copies of books they wish to consider for classroom use. If a school's bookstore has already placed an order for a title, a free desk copy is also available. Please use department letterhead when requesting free books.

Author appearances, virtual or in-person, can often be arranged for book groups, classroom visits, symposia, book fairs, or other educational, literary, or book events.

Visit wtawpress.org for more information.

WTAW Press
PO Box 2825
Santa Rosa, CA 95405
wtaw@wtawpress.org

Printed in the USA
CPSIA information can be obtained
at www.ICGtesting.com
JSHW022145271023
50974JS00005B/185

9 781732 982079